MEREDITH HOOPER was born in Australia, and travelled on a scholarship to do post-graduate study at Nuffield College, Oxford. An historian by training, she is a Visiting Research Fellow in the History of Science at the Royal Institution, and a member of the Association of British Science Writers. She is a prolific author of books which appeal to all ages, including novels, picture books and non-fiction on science, technology and history. Among her previous titles are *A for Antarctica* and *I for Invention* (Piccolo); *How High is the Sky?* (Simon & Schuster); and two books for Frances Lincoln – *The Pebble in my Pocket* (which was the only children's book to be nominated for the History of Science Dingle Book Prize 1997), and *The Drop in my Drink*.

Meredith Hooper has travelled extensively through Europe, the USA, Australia, Antarctica and the Far East. She and her husband have three children, and live in North London.

BERT KITCHEN was born in Liverpool and studied textile design, drawing and painting at the Central School of Art in London. He is now a full-time author and illustrator of children's books. His best-known titles include *Animal Alphabet* and *Animal Numbers*. Bert Kitchen and Meredith Hooper have collaborated on many titles published in the new Cambridge Reading Series.

First published in Great Britain in 1998 by
Frances Lincoln Limited, 4 Torriano Mews
Torriano Avenue, London NW5 2RZ

First paperback edition published in 1999

The author and publishers would like to thank
Robert K. Headland, Archivist and Curator of
the Scott Polar Research Institute, for his help.

British Library Cataloguing in Publication Data
available on request

ISBN 0-7112-1183-3 hardback
ISBN 0-7112-1184-1 paperback

Set in Perpetua

Printed in Hong Kong

9 8 7 6 5 4 3 2 1

*This book is dedicated to the work
of the Antarctic Heritage Trusts.*

TOM'S RABBIT

A True Story from Scott's Last Voyage

MEREDITH HOOPER

Illustrated by BERT KITCHEN

FRANCES LINCOLN

The story in this book really happened, on a voyage
to Antarctica in 1910. The ship was called the Terra Nova.
Her captain was Robert Scott, and Tom Crean,
the sailor, was a member of the crew.

Tom the Sailor picked up Little Rabbit carefully in his big hands. He wrapped her in an old woolly jumper.

"You need a nest, Little Rabbit," said Tom. "Somewhere on this ship there is just the right place — warm and quiet and cosy. Let's go and find it."

Tom the Sailor looked at the black cat with one white whisker. The ship's cat was tucked up in a warm, cosy place. He lay in his own little hammock, just like the sailors' hammocks, with his own little pillow and blanket.

"This hammock is full of black cat," said Tom. "There's no room for you here, Little Rabbit."

Tom the Sailor looked up at the skylight where the ship's parrot was swinging on her perch.

"Hallo, Polly," said Tom.

"Hallo, Polly," said the parrot.

"You can't live on a perch, Little Rabbit," said Tom, and gave the parrot a piece of string to unravel.

Carefully Tom the Sailor climbed down the ladder into the ship's hold. There were boxes and sacks and barrels, in stacks and heaps. It was very cold.

Tom peered around and shivered. "It's much too cold and dark down here for you, Little Rabbit," he said, and climbed back up again quickly.

Tom the Sailor looked into the big cabin. Everyone was busy hanging up paper lanterns, paper chains and flags.

"Come and help us put up the decorations!" they called. "Come on, Tom."

"Not now," said Tom. "I have to find a nest for my rabbit."

Good smells were coming from the galley. Tom looked around the door. The cook was stirring something in a big saucepan.

"What's for dinner?" asked Tom.

"Special surprises for a special dinner," said the cook. "You just wait and see."

Tom the Sailor put on his big, warm jacket. He pulled on his woolly hat and woolly gloves.

"We're going up on deck, Little Rabbit," said Tom. "Mind now, keep warm!"

Snow was falling gently. The sea was covered in big pieces of ice like white meringue. Icebergs floated slowly by, like spiky mountains.

Two whales lifted their great backs in a patch of blue-black water, then sank below the surface.

Fat, silvery seals lay on the ice, yawning and scratching themselves with their flippers. A little group of penguins stood staring at the ship. More penguins scurried across the ice in a long line. One penguin climbed to the top of an ice hill and the others pushed him off.

High above the deck, up against the sky, a wooden barrel was lashed to the mast. Pure white birds flew round and round the rigging.

"It's no good going up there with you, Little Rabbit," said Tom. "You can't climb, and you can't fly."

The deck was filled with dogs. Brown dogs, hairy dogs, black and yellow dogs with pointy ears and curly tails.

Tom tucked Little Rabbit deep inside his jacket.

"Hallo, dogs!" said Tom. The dogs barked and yelped and howled.

Tom the Sailor went forward to the place where the ponies were kept in strong wooden stalls. The ponies were munching oats. They banged at the sides of their stalls with their sharp hooves.

"This ship is full up," said Tom, "it's crammed and crowded. Where can I find you a warm, quiet, cosy place for your nest, Little Rabbit?"

Little Rabbit's long, silky ears drooped.

"I've got it!" shouted Tom suddenly. He ran down eight steps, and poked his head into a gap under the deck where the hay for the ponies was stored. The air smelt sweet.

"Just the place for a nest!" said Tom. Carefully he unwrapped Little Rabbit from the old woolly jumper, and put her on to the hay. Little Rabbit hopped around, sniffed the hay, and lay down.

"And now," said Tom happily, "it's time for my Christmas dinner!"

Everyone sat down around the long table in the big cabin.
They ate . . .

Tomato Soup
Roast Mutton
Plum Pudding
Mince Pies

Then they opened little parcels from their families.
They pulled crackers, and played games, and sang songs.
They were a very long way away from home, but it was
a good Christmas party.

When it was nearly bedtime, Tom went to see if Little Rabbit was all right.

He poked his head into the gap under the deck where the hay was stored. Little Rabbit lay in her warm, cosy nest in the hay. Lying next to her were seventeen baby rabbits.

"That's the best Christmas present ever!" said Tom, happily. "Seventeen babies! Now I can give a rabbit to each of my friends. Well, nearly!"

And he stroked Little Rabbit's long, silky ears.

Tom looked around at the night. The deck was covered in glittering snow. The world was utterly quiet and still. The sun was a soft golden ball, and the ice glowed white, with purple shadows.

"Happy Christmas," said Tom to the world.

The great white continent of Antarctica is surrounded by ice-covered seas.
On Christmas Day, 1910, the Terra Nova was pushing through the ice, towards
land. The men on board, led by Captain Scott, hoped to be the first people to
reach the South Pole. Their husky dogs and ponies would help pull sledges loaded
with food, tents and sleeping bags across the frozen snow.

Tom Crean got close to the South Pole before turning back and helping to save
the life of another explorer. Captain Scott, with four companions, did reach
the Pole, only to find that a Norwegian expedition led by Roald Amundsen had
arrived before them. Scott and his companions died on the return journey.

Tom Crean had many adventures in Antarctica. Along with the explorer, Sir Ernest Shackleton, he sailed a tiny boat across the wild ocean, after the ship Endurance had been crushed in the ice. Later he went back home to Ireland, and ran the South Pole Inn.

The story of Tom's rabbit is based on diaries kept by men on the Terra Nova. Scott wrote in his diary, "An event of Christmas was the production of a family by Crean's rabbit. She gave birth to 17... at present they are warm and snug..."

Meredith Hooper's descriptions of Antarctica are inspired by her travels as a writer with the Australian National Antarctic Research Expedition.

OTHER PICTURE BOOKS IN PAPERBACK FROM FRANCES LINCOLN

THE PEBBLE IN MY POCKET
Meredith Hooper *illustrated by Chris Coady*

Where do pebbles come from? How were they made? Distinguished science writer Meredith Hooper tells the story of a pebble, from its origins in a fiery volcano 480 million years ago, to its place in a busy, modern landscape. 'Perfect for a child who likes to know exactly when, why and how' — *The Guardian*

Suitable for National Curriculum English — Reading, Key Stages 2 and 3; Science, Key Stages 2 and 3
Scottish Guidelines English Language — Reading, Level D; Environmental Studies, Level D

ISBN 0-7112-1076-4   £4.99

CAMILLE AND THE SUNFLOWERS
Laurence Anholt

"One day a strange man arrived in Camille's town. He had a straw hat and a yellow beard…" The strange man is the artist Vincent van Gogh, seen through the eyes of a young boy entranced by Vincent's painting. An enchanting introduction to the great painter, with reproduction of Van Gogh's work.

Suitable for National Curriculum English — Reading, Key Stages 1 and 2; Art, Key Stage 2
Scottish Guidelines English Language — Reading, Levels B and C; Art and Design, Levels B and C

ISBN 0-7112-1050-0   £4.99

MY NAPOLEON
Catherine Brighton

When Betsy Balcombe learns that the former Emperor Napoleon Bonaparte is coming to stay at her father's house on the island of St Helena, she imagines a demon with a long pointed tail. But they get on famously. Catherine Brighton's story, based on Betsy's memoirs published in 1855, perfectly portrays the spirit of childhood.

Suitable for National Curriculum English — Reading, Key Stage 2
Scottish Guidelines English Language — Reading, Levels B and C; Environmental Studies, Levels B and C

ISBN 0-7112-1127-2   £4.99

Frances Lincoln titles are available at all good bookshops.
Prices and availablilty are correct at time of publication but may be subject to change.